IGNORED
and
Treasured

THE DUKE'S BOOKISH BRIDE

BY
BREE WOLF

Cover Art by Victoria Cooper
Copyright © 2018 Bree Wolf

Paperback ISBN: 978-3-96482-063-1
Hardcover ISBN: 978-3-96482-115-7

www.breewolf.com

To my most devoted readers
Thank you for sharing my novels with friends and family
and helping more readers find these stories

Acknowledgments

This prequel to my Love's Second Chance Series is meant as a thank-you to all of you who have supported me through your wonderful feedback, by sharing your thoughts and recommending my novels to other readers, by posting heartfelt reviews and sending me smiley faces when I needed them, by encouraging others to buy my books and give me a chance.

Thank you for everything you do every day!

IGNORED *and* Treasured

Prologue

London 1750 (or a variation thereof)

A gentle smile on her lips, Margot Archer, Countess of Hargreaves, looked down upon her young daughter. "You looked beautiful tonight," she whispered as they stood outside Helen's chamber. "Did you enjoy your debut?"

Helen sighed, seeing hope shining in her mother's kind eyes. "I did," she replied, willing the smile to remain on her lips for a moment longer. "It was...magical." Is that not what her younger sister Sophie would have called such an evening? Magical?

"I'm glad." Squeezing her daughter's hand, the countess arched her brows. "I'm certain you'll find a husband before the season is out, my dear."

Unable to answer, Helen merely continued to smile.

"Good night, my dear," her mother whispered before she headed down the hallway toward her own bedchamber.

Once her mother had disappeared from sight, Helen allowed the muscles in her face to relax. Entering her room, she shifted her jaw from side to side to dispel the ache that had come to her face from constant smiling. Did anyone truly enjoy this?

Allowing her maid to remove the dress and let down her hair, Helen then quickly sent the young woman to bed, seeing no need to keep her up. After spending an evening surrounded by too many people to begin with, Helen longed to have her thoughts to herself. Peace and quiet was exactly what she needed to relieve the tender throbbing under her temples. Why on earth would anyone choose to attend balls?

After all, they were so loud, the air filled with laughter and idle chit-chat. Stuffy and overcrowded, the ballroom had brought on an almost desperate wish to open not only one but all the windows available as Helen's lungs had strained to suck in what remained of fresh air.

Oh, what she would not have given to have been allowed to stay home that night, snuggled up in bed with a good book!

Sinking into her pillows, Helen sighed, her eyes beginning to close. Unfortunately, peace and quiet would have to wait a bit longer, for in that moment her younger sister Sophie-younger by one year-burst through the door.

"You're back!" she exclaimed, rushing to scramble up onto the bed. "Tell me everything!"

Again, Helen sighed. "And you're still up," she observed, watching her sister climb under the blanket. "Why?"

Sophie stared at her blankly, her chestnut curls framing a soft face. "How could I possibly sleep?" she asked, incredulity in her voice.

Helen shrugged. "Try lying down and closing your eyes. That usually works for me."

Sophie laughed, "Oh, don't jest! Please, tell me everything! Who did you dance with? Did anyone catch your eye? What did it feel like to be swept across the dance floor?"

Seeing the eagerness in her sister's face, Helen did not have the heart to tell her the truth. Sophie had always been a romantic, prone to seeing life as a fairy tale. "It was...magical," she began and was rewarded by a girlish shriek as Sophie clapped her hands together in delight, her green eyes sparkling even in the dim light of the room. "The food was...exquisite. Everyone was dressed in their finest. I enjoyed..." Oh, there had to have been something? "...the music. It was quite nice, and I shall look forward to hearing it again."

Concentrating on what to say, Helen only belatedly realised that the enthusiastic glow on her sister's face had dimmed, replaced by a slight frown. "You had an awful time, didn't you?"

Helen sighed, "I'm sorry. I tried," she assured her sister. "I truly and honestly tried, but it was simply not my idea of an entertaining evening. I'm sorry."

An indulgent smile played on Sophie's lips as she looked at her elder sister. "How will you ever find your match if you do not mingle?"

Helen shrugged. "I'm not certain I ever do want to find a match." In truth, Helen had decided long ago that she would not marry.

For one, she was far from a beauty and generally failed to attract men's attentions. Her brown hair was rather ordinary, missing the sparkling nuances her sister possessed, while her face had *too much character* as her late grandfather had called it, his disapproval clear in the way he had looked at her.

Always had Helen thought it a cruel sense of irony that she had been the first born and thus received the name Helen, after Helen of Troy.

The face that launched a thousand ships.

Almost obsessed with ancient texts and cultures, her father had chosen meaningful names as he called them for his two daughters. Unfortunately, he had chosen them in the wrong order, and so the plain first-born girl had ended up with a name that spoke of great beauty, whereas, her younger sister had been named for the *wisdom* their father treasured in life.

Not that Sophie was not wise in her own ways. However, as the bookish sister, Helen had always thought they should simply switch their names in order to avoid giving people the wrong impression and be thus held to unrealistic expectations.

The other reason for her desire to remain unmarried was simply that Helen knew she had very little in common with *others*. Whenever she opened her mouth and spoke of things that mattered to her, like history, philosophy and ancient cultures, people would look at her with unveiled disapproval as well as incomprehension. The only way for Helen to avoid these looks was to remain silent.

And Helen refused to live a life where she was met by either disapproval or had to refrain from expressing her thoughts in order to avoid it.

Therefore, marriage had never seemed an option. At least not for her.

"Do not think so lowly of yourself, dear sister," Sophie chided. "You are a remarkable young woman. However, for others to notice, you need to give them the opportunity to do so."

Smiling at her younger sister lovingly, Helen sighed, knowing that despite her exuberant ways, Sophie had a very loyal heart. "I assure you," Helen began, "that I do not think lowly of myself. Quite on the contrary. I do not wish to change merely to catch a husband, and so far, all English society has done is prove that there is none who would want me for who I am. Therefore, it is only reasonable to conclude that marriage is not for me. Can you not see that?"

Rolling her eyes, Sophie shook her head. "Not at all. Let me ask you this: Have you met *all* of society?"

Helen inhaled a deep breath. "I've met enough of society to know that-"

"To suspect," Sophie interrupted, a triumphant gleam in her eyes. "I admit you are...a rare specimen." A teasing smile came to her lips. "Would it then not also be logical to assume that your perfect match is an equally rare specimen and, therefore, not easy to discover?"

Sighing, Helen shook her head. "You do possess a unique kind of wisdom, dear Sophie."

Leaning in conspiratorially, her sister whispered, "I am aware. Then tell me, what is holding you back? So that I can impart some more of my unique wisdom."

Helen chuckled, then shrugged. "I cannot say. I simply think it is a waste of time to search for someone who in all likelihood does not even exist."

"Oh, I'm certain he does exist," Sophie objected. "All you need to do is look for a face that looks as bored as your own, and then you'll have found him." Giggling, Sophie hid her face in the pillows before coming up for breath.

Unexpectedly, Sophie's silly description conjured the image of a man with dark hair and even darker eyes. He had stood off to the side and not participated in the dancing and general merriment of the evening.

"You saw someone like that, didn't you?" Sophie exclaimed, her eyes shining with excitement.

Feeling an unfamiliar heat creep up her cheeks, Helen quickly averted her gaze. It would not serve her well to encourage her sister, certain if she did, she would never hear the end of it.

"You cannot hide how you feel, dear sister," Sophie chided. "You never could. It's written all over your face. You've found someone who could be the one for you. Then go and get him."

Helen's jaw dropped. "Go and get him?" she repeated, momentarily too stunned to form a coherent thought.

Sophie shrugged. "It's what I would do." Again, she leaned forward conspiratorially. "Before someone else snatches him up."

Helen laughed. "You are not me, and I do believe I shall dance at your wedding before you dance at mine...if at all."

Crossing her arms in front of her, Sophie shook her head. "I vow that I shall not marry before you. So, you see, if you wish for me to be happy, you'll need to find your own true love first."

Once again, Helen's jaw dropped. "You cannot do this. Think of your own happiness."

"I am, for I know I shall never be happy if you are not also."

Shaking her head, Helen squeezed her sister's hand. "You are my dearest friend, but I advise you to marry whomever catches your heart and not make your happiness dependent on me."

"That is excellent advice," Sophie said, kissing Helen good night before she scrambled out of bed. "You should do so as well." Grinning, Sophie stepped out into the hallway to return to her own chamber.

Helen sank back into her pillows, remembering the stranger's darkened look. Had he truly disliked the event as much as she? And was that any sign that they were at all compatible?

Shaking her head, Helen knew that although her sister meant well, she was still too innocent in the ways of the world to know what marriage meant.

In all likelihood, there was not a single man in London who would like Helen for whom she was and desire her to be his wife.

Such a man did not exist, at least not one whom Helen would choose also.

Chapter One
LADY SOPHIE'S DEBUT

London 1751 (or a variation thereof)

One Year Later

"Oh, I can't believe tonight is finally here!" Sophie exclaimed, her hands curling into fists as she tried to control the trembling that shook her body. "This is a dream come true!"

Smiling, Helen looked from her sister seated next to her across the carriage at their parents. Both had the same delight shining in their eyes as they beheld their daughter's joy at her first ball. Exchanging a look with her husband, their mother seemed to lean closer toward him, a gesture of devotion and trust as well as comfort and familiarity. Helen often marvelled at the deep bond that existed between her parents.

"Your eyes shine like stars, my dear," their mother observed as she leaned forward and gently squeezed Sophie's hand. "You look radiant tonight."

"Thank you, Mother," Sophie whispered, inhaling a deep breath as she tried her best to calm her nerves.

A slight frown came to their mother's face as she turned her gaze to Helen. "I cannot help but remember," she began, a teasing note in her voice, "that you didn't seem half as enthusiastic as your sister does now."

Helen shrugged, knowing that in a tight-knit family as theirs she would not be able to fool anyone if she were to disagree. "What can I say, Mother? I never favoured dancing."

Sophie chuckled, "You may not get enthusiastic about balls, dear sister, but I've seen you this enthusiastic before."

Their mother's brows crinkled into a frown.

"Upon discovering a book," Sophie exclaimed, her own nerves forgotten as she teased her sister. "Do not pretend you don't have this kind of passion within you!"

Helen shrugged. "Which book was it?"

Sophie shook her head. "I have no idea."

"I'm afraid that I am to blame for this," their father chuckled as he met Helen's gaze. "You are too much like me, preferring a good book over a social occasion. I'm afraid I never felt at ease at balls and, therefore, rarely attended."

Laughing, their mother took her husband's hand in hers. "Still, you cannot deny that it was one such social occasion that brought us together. If you had never attended," she whispered, her eyes shining as she looked at him, "we would never have met."

Their father nodded, a soft smile playing on his lips. "You're too right, my love. I never once regretted attending that night. On the contrary, it was the night my life began."

"Oh, I wish I could find what you two have," Sophie sighed, pulling Helen's arm through hers as she hugged her close. "Don't you agree?"

Opening her mouth, Helen did not know how to reply. Although their parents shared a deep love, they were opposites in almost every way. And yet, there was a calmness between them as though they were one, and not two people with opposing thoughts. Deep down, Helen admitted that she longed to know what their secret was.

Ignoring her sister's lack of a reply, Sophie turned eager eyes back to their parents. "You're so different. How did you know you would suit?"

After exchanging another meaningful look with her husband, their mother turned to them, a peaceful smile on her face. "Of course, we didn't know. There is no knowing, no certainty. Having common ground certainly helps, but whether or not two people suit is not about having the same interests. Differences, too, can present quite an opportunity to learn and grow, to open one's horizon." Smiling, she squeezed her husband's hand. "What I found most important is to not only feel excited about the one you are with, but to also feel at ease. To feel safe. At home. Perfectly content."

Sighing, Sophie looked at Helen as their parents turned their attention toward one another. "I do hope I will be as happy as they are one day."

"I hope that, too," Helen mumbled, certain that if anyone had a chance of finding true happiness, it was her sister. After all, her sweetness and dedication made her a rare woman. Any man would be fortunate to win her heart!

Chapter Two

CHOOSING A BRIDE

Alexander Astor, Duke of Kensington, was bored out of his mind.

Certainly, the music was pleasant, the temperature bearable and the food intriguing. However, Alexander could not help but feel annoyed by the charade that manifested before his eyes whenever he dared set foot into a ballroom.

As rare an occurrence as that was.

Dressed up in their finest, ladies paraded around the room, trying their best to catch the attention of a certain gentleman while in turn the gentlemen in attendance prowled the premises like predators on the hunt. Their smiles and words seemed dishonest, only meant to create the illusion of a desirable match. Whether or not, two people actually did suit was a far cry from what passed as truthful at these events.

Alexander knew it would be another tedious evening, and he longed for the peace and quiet of his library. The only reason he had come here tonight had been his mother's insistence that he *finally choose a bride*. Not that he had any intention of binding himself to a woman whose company he already found tedious after only a short acquaintance. He would be a fool to do so.

However, attending a ball every once in a while kept up appearances and placated his mother.

After Alexander had done his duty and conversed a little here and there, renewed an acquaintance and danced at least once, he felt at ease to leave the noisy crowd behind and venture into a quieter part of the house. Not that he had a particular interest in art or antiques; however, the life that hid behind these objects intrigued him.

Stopping in front of an ancient cup with a deep bowl, tall pedestal-foot and a pair of high-swung handles, Alexander noted that it was adorned with images of people and vines as though a celebration was being held. Curious, he marvelled at the people who had once used it in their lives. Had this been a regular drinking vessel? Or had it been made for special occasions only?

"Oh!"

The soft exclamation made him straighten and turn to face whoever had discovered his absence. Annoyed to have been found, Alexander searched for an adequate excuse to explain why he was wandering through the house instead of attending the dance. However, when his gaze fell on the young lady who stood in the doorway, he suddenly found himself at a loss.

Dressed in a simple gown with few adornments, her eyes shone brightly as they beheld him. Unexpectedly, they held no sign of disapproval, but rather a hint of surprise mixed with a touch of understanding as though she, too, had sought a reprieve from the noise of the crowded ballroom. Clutched in her hands, she held a book.

"I'm sorry to disturb you, my lord," she all but whispered, her voice almost reverent as though she wished not to disturb the peace and quiet of the room.

"I do not mind," Alexander heard himself saying. "I'm not quite certain what I'm looking at in any case."

Hugging the book to her chest, she took a step forward, a hint of curiosity in her dark green eyes. "You seemed quite absorbed for someone without an interest in artefacts, or am I mistaken?"

"You are not," Alexander admitted, taking a step back from the artful cup and closer to the intriguing, young lady. "However, I do believe a lack in knowledge always presents an opportunity to learn."

At his words, a soft smile came to her lips, and Alexander could not help but think that she was pleased. "Is that so? Would you care to learn then?" she asked, her eyes lighting up with challenge. "Would a mere cup interest you?"

"It would," he replied, "if only there were someone who could instruct me." Holding her emerald eyes, Alexander realised that he was indeed enjoying the pleasure of her company. "Am I correct to assume that you are in possession of the necessary knowledge to do so?"

For a moment, her eyes darkened, and there seemed to be a touch of doubt in the way she looked at him. However, it passed quickly, and her face took on a look of restrained eagerness as she stepped towards him. "You would indeed assume right." Coming to stand beside him, she shifted her gaze from his and looked down at the cup, her eyes tracing the images almost lovingly. "This is called a cantharus. It is from ancient Greece and was used for drinking as well as as a banqueting cup for pagan rituals." For a moment, her eyes lingered on his as she hesitated to continue.

Alexander wondered if she doubted him before recalling that men generally disliked knowledgeable females. For a reason he could not understand, many of his peers sought wives with a pretty face and an empty head. Did they fear to be challenged? He wondered. But was that not the spark of life? To be challenged? To be allowed to learn and grow?

Apparently, she did not detect any signs of disapproval or boredom on his face for she continued in her instructions. "The images are associated with Dionysus, the Greek god of wine. He is generally associated with vegetation and fertility."

"I see," was all Alexander could manage as his gaze lingered on hers, more than intrigued by her bright intelligent eyes and the wisdom that shone on her face. This was indeed a woman who did not shy away from books, from learning, from the knowledge they provided. Still, as she continued to point out other artefacts around the room, Alexander noticed not only an eagerness to converse and share what she knew, but also doubt.

At first, Alexander had thought she was concerned by the fact that they were indeed alone. However, her gaze never ventured toward the door as though fearing to be discovered. Instead, it seemed to linger on his face, trying to look deeper as though she feared to bore him or tried to gauge whether or not he disapproved of her instructions.

And yet, she continued on, not trying to hide the commendable mind she possessed.

"I'm sorry," she said, a slight chuckle escaping her lips. "I've said much, not giving you the opportunity to contribute to this conversation."

Shaking his head, Alexander waved her concerns away. "I did not mind. Clearly, in this regard, your education is far superior to my own."

A slight blush came to her cheeks, and yet, her eyes seemed to gather in brightness, shining like two stars in the night sky. "My father's passions are ancient cultures and all they taught, all they can still teach us today."

"And you join in his efforts to learn?" Alexander inquired, wondering why he had never noticed her before. Then again, he had rarely attended any social gatherings throughout the last season and had had no intention of changing that this season...at least not until now.

Grinning, she bit her lower lip, delight obvious on her face. "I suppose the apple does not fall far from the tree. At least not in my case."

Arching his brows, Alexander looked at her expectantly, realising that he wished to know all he could about this rare woman.

Shaking her head, she laughed, "My sister is not at all like me."

"And yet you are very close," Alexander replied, holding her gaze as he tried to see if he was mistaken.

Her eyes narrowed a fraction as she cocked her head a little, regarding him with interest...and possibly a hint of suspicion. "Have we met before?"

Alexander shook his head. "We have not. Of that I am certain." The soft smile that came to her lips did not escape him. "However, the way you speak of her reminds me of my own two sisters. Opposites in every way, and yet, no one has ever come between them." He chuckled. "Not even their husbands."

Holding his gaze openly, she laughed, and the sound echoed gently through the large room, finer than any music Alexander had ever perceived. "Is it the same with brothers?" she asked then. "Are you in a position to know?"

A bit saddened, Alexander shook his head, remembering his childhood when he had always felt like the one missing his other half. "I'm afraid not."

Her eyes dimmed a little, and her smile softened as though she was very well aware of the regret that clung to his answer. "Sometimes a friend can be like a brother," she suggested, her gaze open, waiting.

Drawn to her by the secrets that seemed to pass between them so easily, Alexander took a step closer, his gaze remaining on hers. "I'm afraid I'm not a sociable man. Forming new acquaintances easily is not a skill I possess."

For a moment, she glanced down at the book she still held clutched to her chest before her eyes rose to meet his, a soft smile playing on her features. "Neither do I. I find I have very little in common with...others."

Mesmerized by the depth of her eyes, Alexander nodded.

As the moments stretched on, she blinked, her gaze darting beyond his shoulder before she inhaled a deep breath, a hint of awareness colouring her cheeks. "I thought I was the only one trying to escape these events."

Alexander smiled. "I assure you, you are not. I-" Distant voices echoed to their ears in that moment, and he saw her eyes widen at the sudden realisation that they found themselves in a rather compromising situation.

"I need to return," she whispered, her gaze shifting around the room as though looking for a way out.

Holding out his hand, Alexander felt his heart skip a beat when she slid hers into his own without a moment of hesitation. Gently, he urged her away from the door and behind a large case holding more antiques he could not name.

Outside, the voices drifted closer, and Alexander could make out a man speaking to a woman. However, he failed to detect what they were saying. Instead, he was very much aware of the woman standing only an inch away from him, her back pressed against the wall, her breath coming fast as she tried to peek around the case blocking her view.

"All will be well," he assured her, suddenly consumed by the desire to see her safe, to protect her.

At the sound of his voice, she raised her head and her lips almost brushed his.

A jolt went through Alexander, and before he knew what was happening, he had already pulled her into his arms. His gaze held hers, and he felt her soft breath against his lips. Then she tilted her head a fraction higher, and it was all the encouragement he needed.

Claiming her mouth, he kissed her gently, oddly aware of the book lodged between them like a barrier keeping them apart.

In the stillness of the room, the door they had left ajar closed with a deafening thud, and both their heads snapped up. Glancing around the room, Alexander tried to determine if anyone had entered without their noticing. After all, they had been...distracted.

Fortunately, it seemed as though the door had been closed from the outside.

"I need to get back," she whispered beside him as she stepped forward, her eyes searching the room as though she still doubted that they were indeed alone.

"I shall see you b-"

Before he could finish his sentence, she darted to the door, cracked it open and peered outside. Then she stepped out into the hallway and disappeared from his sight.

Hurrying after her, Alexander tried his best to shake off the daze that had consumed him at her closeness. However, by the time he reached the door and looked outside, she was nowhere to be seen. Knowing that she had wanted to return to the ballroom, Alexander strode in the same direction.

The noise rushed at him with an almost painful intensity, and he had to slow his steps in order to regain his composure. Standing back off to the side, he then let his gaze sweep the large room, his heart clenching painfully when he failed to detect her right away.

Still, after a few moments of excruciating doubt and uncertainty, his gaze finally beheld her as she stood across the room from him, speaking to another young woman. Their heads were inclined to one another in confidence and only snapped up when an older couple approached.

"She's a rare woman, is she not?"

Startled out of his thoughts, Alexander turned to find Pierce Dunsworth, Duke of Cromwell, standing beside him, a smug grin plastered on the man's face.

"I suppose," Alexander mumbled, not in the least inclined to discuss any kind of personal matter with a known rake, unable to show discretion if his life depended on it.

"You suppose?" Cromwell laughed. "I would say she is one of a kind. A woman one stumbles upon perhaps once in a lifetime." His voice sobered. "I tell you she will be married before the season is out."

Gritting his teeth, Alexander felt a rather unfamiliar desire to pound Cromwell into the ground when he realised that possibly for the first time in the man's life, he showed true interest in a woman. "Are you well acquainted?" he asked instead, doing his best to hold on to his composure.

"Not yet," Cromwell grinned, a longing sigh following his words. "However, I am determined to win Lady Sophie's heart," he turned to look at Alexander, "as well as her hand."

Meeting the man's gaze, Alexander did not fail to detect the challenge that had already rung in his voice. "I wish you good luck, Cromwell."

A grin spread over the man's face. "To you as well. May the best man win." Then he turned and strode away.

Briefly, Alexander closed his eyes and inhaled a deep breath, willing his tense muscles to relax. When he opened them once more, his gaze unerringly returned to...Lady Sophie. What a fitting name!

Indeed, she was brilliant and wise and utterly unique!

If only Cromwell had not noticed her as well.

Again, his mother's words echoed in his mind, only now they no longer sounded like a chore or a threat or an ultimatum. Excitement coursed through his body at the thought of pursuing Lady Sophie.

Perhaps he ought to call on her.
Soon.
Before he lost her to Cromwell.

Chapter Three
A MAGICAL NIGHT

He had kissed her!

Apparently, it was the only thought Helen's mind was capable of that night. Not only did she fail to take note of anything beyond the man's dark eyes as they returned to meet hers again and again, but she was also oblivious to the fact that she had not even gotten his name.

Only once they were seated in their carriage on their way back home did realisation dawn on Helen. and she impulsively clasped a hand over her mouth, startling the rest of her family into inquiring about her health. While her parents seemed reassured after her ludicrous explanation of a hairpin getting loose and pinching her, Helen knew that her sister was not that easily fooled. For the remainder of the ride home, Sophie's gaze remained on her, a hint of suspicion in her dark green eyes.

And so, it was no surprise at all when not long after Helen had retired, the door once more burst open and Sophie strolled in, a prematurely triumphant smile on her face. Once more, she climbed into Helen's bed and snuggled into the pillows. "How did you like it tonight?" she asked simply, and yet, Helen knew that Sophie would not leave the room until she had the answer she sought.

Unwilling to share her secret just yet, Helen chose to at least try and protect the unexpected treasure she had found that night.

He had kissed her!

"It was quite nice," Helen replied to her sister's question. "I assume these are not the words you would use. I saw the smile that hung on your face all evening."

A sigh escaped Sophie's lips as she sunk deeper into the pillows. "It was magical," she breathed, her thoughts at least momentarily distracted. "Like a fairy tale. I felt like Cinderella at her ball meeting her prince."

"Her prince?" Helen pressed, remembering the blond-haired, young lord who had never ventured far from her sister's side. Although most persistent, he had only been one of many. As expected, Sophie's debut had been a roaring success, and it seemed all the men of London were now taken with her little sister. She would certainly have her choice of husbands.

"Indeed," Sophie whispered, a conspiratorial twinkle in her eyes. "I danced with many handsome and gallant gentlemen tonight. However, there was one who..." She sighed. "The way he smiled at me made me weak in the knees."

"Who was he?"

Some of the dreaminess vanished from Sophie's voice. "To tell you the truth, I think he is a bit of a rake."

"A rake?" Helen exclaimed, slightly alarmed.

"Don't worry, dear sister," Sophie assured her. "I shall not allow him to fool me. If he is indeed interested, then he shall have to prove himself." With a grin on her face, she met Helen's gaze. "I am determined to make him work for me, to show that he truly cares for me."

"That seems wise," Helen replied, relieved to hear that her impulsive, little sister had a clever head upon her young shoulders.

"And what of you?" Sophie asked, turning the conversation around. "Did you meet anyone?"

Helen cringed. She had never been good at lying, and beyond anything, she disliked lying to her sister. Turning her head, she tried to think of something that would not be a lie while not revealing her secret at the same time. For a reason, she could not name, Helen did not wish for anyone to know.

Not even Sophie.

Sitting up, Sophie looked down at her, her gaze narrowed, a hint of suspicion back in her eyes. "Something happened tonight, didn't it?" she demanded, her gaze sweeping over Helen's face as though she knew how to read it like a book. "For part of the evening, I could not find you anywhere. You seemed to have disappeared."

Feigning nonchalance, Helen chuckled. "I'm surprised you noticed with all the dancing you did."

"Don't try to change the subject, dear sister," Sophie warned. "I know I'm distracted easily, but not where you're concerned. Tell me. Where did you go?"

Relieved to hear her sister ask such a simple question, Helen sat up as well, trying her best to hold Sophie's inquisitive gaze. "Nowhere in particular," she said with a shrug of her shoulders. "I simply looked around the house. Apparently, the Dashwood's are great collectors. In one room, I found a cantharus from ancient Greece. It had the most beautiful-"

Holding up a hand, Sophie silenced her. "Don't even try to bore me with your artefacts. I'm not *that* easily distracted." Leaning forward, Sophie's gaze narrowed. "Now more than ever, I'm convinced that you did meet someone. Perhaps-" Her eyes widened. "Did he find you there? In the room with the antiques?"

Swallowing a gulp of air, Helen shook her head. "No, he did not." After all, it was *she* who had found *him*. So, this was not technically a lie, was it?

"Helen!" Sophie warned, her voice rising as she crossed her arms in front of her chest. "I know you're hiding something. What happened?"

He had kissed her!

"Don't make me draw it out of you!" Sophie pressed. "I assure you you won't like it, and I shall know the truth in any case."

Helen frowned, starting to get annoyed. "This is none of your concern."

"Aha!" Sophie exclaimed, a look of triumph on her face. "I knew it! Who did you meet?"

Sighing in resignation, Helen stacked up her pillows and sat back against the headboard. "I don't know," she whispered. "I never got his name."

Sophie frowned, clearly disappointed by Helen's retelling. "Why not? Did you not speak?"

"We did," Helen admitted, remembering the open joy in his eyes as she had shared her knowledge with him. No one had ever quite looked at her that way. At least not a man. At least not a man who was not her father.

"What about?"

"Artefacts," Helen stressed, meeting her sister's gaze. "Remember the cantharus I mentioned a moment ago. It had-"

"Yes, I remember," Sophie cut her off, a hint of disappointment coming to her face. "That's all you did? Talk of antiques?"

Unintentionally, Helen's thoughts strayed to the moment they had hidden behind the large case of artefacts. The moment his arms had come around her. The moment he had kissed her.

Instantly, heat shot up her cheeks before she could prevent it.

Sophie's mouth dropped open and her eyes widened in utter delight. "I knew it!" she exclaimed once more. "Tell me! Did he kiss you?"

Closing her eyes, Helen exhaled a slow breath. Then she met her sister's softened gaze. "He did."

"And?" Sophie pressed gently.

Helen could not quite keep the smile off her face. "It was…magical," she said for lack of a better word. "He seemed as out of place at the ball as I was. He listened to what I said; he seemed to want to. He seemed to enjoy it."

With a large smile on her face, Sophie sighed in delight. "He seems to be the very man for you. Have you never seen him before?"

Helen shook her head, then froze. "Perhaps once. At my own debut, I saw him across the room."

"And?"

"Nothing," Helen assured her sister. "I never saw him again."

Sophie grinned. "And yet, you remembered seeing him then? He must have made quite the impression."

"He did," Helen whispered, her thoughts drawn back to the stranger who had so unexpectedly touched her heart. Never had Helen thought she would fall in love. Especially not like this. Not in the course of one evening. And yet, she could not deny that the memory of their shared moments did something to her heart that she had never experienced before. Was this love? Or the precursor that would lead to love?

"Do you wish to see him again?" Sophie asked, a wide grin on her face.

Helen smiled. "I believe so." Then she drew in a slow breath. "What if *he* does not?"

Sophie shook her head. "I'm certain he does. After all, he kissed you, did he not?"

Helen scoffed, "Despite our limited experience, we are both well aware that a kiss is not always born out of deep affection, especially for a man. It might simply have been...the magic of the moment. Nothing more." Helen sighed, "At least for him." Raising her gaze to meet Sophie's, Helen tried her best to dissuade her enthusiastic sister lest she succeed in raising Helen's hopes...only to have them plummet into a dark hole. "At least, *you* have a whole circle of admirers to choose from."

Shaking her head, Sophie rolled her eyes. "It does not matter how many suitors either one of us has, for it only takes one man to make us truly happy. Even with a long list of suitors, I can only choose one husband, and he better be the one who unhinges my world with a single look." Reaching out, Sophie grasped Helen's hand. "Don't be discouraged. I know you have a tendency of discouraging yourself because you fear the pain of disappointed hopes. But don't let true love slip through your fingers because you fear to reach for it."

A gentle smile came to Helen's face as her heart grew lighter. "You are indeed wise, dear sister. What would I do without you?"

Sophie laughed, "Not go to the next ball, I'm certain. Be assured, I'll not allow you to miss it."

"I don't even know he will be there," Helen objected. "It seems he rarely attends."

"That's all the more reason to go," Sophie concluded, another triumphant smile flashing across her face. "If he does attend, it will almost certainly be for the reason of seeing you." Looking at her indulgently, Sophie asked, "Will you promise to go?"

Sighing, Helen nodded. "I promise."

A shriek of joy tore from Sophie's lips as she jumped up and clapped her hands together. "Oh, we will have such a marvellous time!" Then she kissed Helen good night and rushed from the room, no doubt towards dreams of her very own Prince Charming.

Closing her eyes, Helen recalled the bright and interested gaze of the stranger she had met that night. He had been so focused on her as though he had truly enjoyed listening to her. And then he had kissed her! Could Sophie be right?

Did he care for her?

Helen hoped with all her heart that her sister was not mistaken.

Chapter Four

TO CALL ON A LADY

A few days after the ball at the Dashwood townhouse, Alexander finally decided to throw caution to the wind and call on Lady Sophie. After all, if Cromwell had honest intentions toward her, there was no time to lose.

After being shown to the drawing room, Alexander wandered from one cabinet to the next, inspecting the antiques portrayed proudly. Indeed, Lady Sophie's father was a dedicated collector. No wonder his daughter was following in the man's footsteps.

Upon hearing the door opening in his back, Alexander straightened and inhaled a slow breath. Then he turned, his gaze straining to find the set of bright, intelligent eyes that had so held him captive. Unfortunately, the eyes he met were not the ones he had sought. Certainly, they were green as well, but they did not affect him, did not touch his heart the way they had at the ball.

Alexander blinked.

By the door stood a young woman with bright features and a kind smile, a hint of speculation in her eyes as she looked at him. Unfortunately, this woman was not the one he had hoped to meet.

"Good day, Lord Kensington," she greeted him. "Please have a seat."

Sinking into the nearest chair, Alexander could barely keep himself from staring at her as though he feared his eyes were deceiving him. Belatedly, he remembered to mumble a greeting in return. His conscious mind barely took note of the maid who had entered silently and began arranging flowers in a vase.

After seating herself across from him on the settee, she watched him, her green eyes darkening in confusion. "I admit I am rather surprised that you would call on me," she said openly, "as I do not believe we have yet been introduced. Or am I wrong?"

Clearing his throat, Alexander was at a loss. "You're not, my lady. And I apologise if I overstepped. I suppose I should take my leave." Just when he was about to rise, the door opened wider and in walked the woman he had been yearning to see again for the past few days.

"Sophie, I was wondering if you'd like-" The moment she perceived him, her voice broke off and her eyes widened as she stopped in her tracks.

Shooting to his feet, Alexander stared at her, feeling his heart awaken at the very sight of her. His pulse thudded in his veins, and he could barely keep himself from striding forward. For a bare moment, he thought to see a flicker of joy in her eyes before they darted to the young woman on the settee. Instantly, her features darkened, and she swallowed. "I'm sorry to intrude."

"Not at all," Lady Sophie assured her. "Let me introduce you to Lord Kensington. Lord Kensington, this is my-"

"I'm sorry," she interrupted, her eyes downcast as she backed out of the room. "I'm...I need to go." Then she spun around and hurried away.

Taking a step toward the door, Alexander wished he could go after her. However, his sense of decorum forbade him to do so, and so reluctantly, he turned back to Lady Sophie.

Her eyes were slightly narrowed as her gaze moved from the door back to him. "Well, that *was* my sister Helen." Her brows crinkled further. "Have you ever made her acquaintance?"

Helen! Her sister Helen!

Remembering the moment Cromwell had stepped up to him at the ball, Alexander could have groaned. Had the man given him the wrong name deliberately? Had he tried to hinder Alexander's pursuit?

Realising that Lady Sophie had asked him a question, Alexander swallowed, trying to concentrate. "I believe so," he said, his voice strained. "At the Dashwood ball."

At his answer, Lady Sophie's eyes widened before a contemplative look came to her gaze. "Is that so? Well, I cannot say I've seen the two of you together. Did you dance?"

His thoughts still occupied with Cromwell's dishonourable conduct, Alexander said, "We did not. Your sister enlightened me on a few rare artefacts in Lord Dashwood's collection."

A smile curled up Lady Sophie's lips as though she had been able to finally puzzle out a riddle. "That sounds delightful," she exclaimed, her eyes gliding over him in rather frank perusal. "I wish I could have been there." For a moment, her gaze became distant as though she was mulling something over. Then, however, her eyes returned to his, and her features grew more animated. "I must say I do enjoy your company, my lord. You are such a skilled conversationalist."

A bit confused, Alexander stared at her as she tried to draw him into a conversation. Certain that his lack of enthusiasm should have been discouraging to the lady, he was even more surprised when she appeared to be batting her lashes at him.

Was he going mad? Or losing his eyesight? Why would a woman treated with the very indifference he was currently portraying show any kind of interest in him?

"It is such pleasant weather," she exclaimed. "Utterly perfect for riding through Hyde Park, wouldn't you agree, my lord?"

Alexander nodded, belatedly realising that she was hinting for an invitation and wished for him to invite her on an outing. He sighed, knowing that all this had been his fault...if not Cromwell's! After all, *he*, Alexander, had been the one to call on *her* and thus given her the wrong impression with regard to his intentions. Guilt swept through his heart, and before he could stop himself, he offered to escort her on a ride through Hyde Park the next day.

"Marvellous!" Lady Sophie exclaimed. "I am certain it shall be a day worth remembering."

Realising his mistake too late, Alexander gritted his teeth. After all, all his invitation had managed to accomplish was to encourage the lady's interest and assure her of his own. He was a blasted fool!

If Lady Sophie were to come to care for him, he could never end that courtship and still hope to win Helen's heart. From his own experience, he knew very well that sisters were often loyal to a fault. If he were to break Lady Sophie's heart, Helen would never accept him. How on earth had he ended up in this mess?

Finally taking his leave-something he should have done long before now! - Alexander felt his heart cringe at the predicament he found himself in. Still lost in a sense of devastation, he barely noticed Cromwell striding toward him through the entry foyer.

Grinning, the man greeted him. "I see your intentions are equally persistent as my own." Stopping in front of Alexander, Cromwell leaned forward and whispered once again, "May the best man win." Then he winked at him and before Alexander had recovered his wits strode toward Lady Sophie and greeted her enthusiastically.

In that moment, Alexander finally realised what had landed him in his current predicament, and he closed his eyes, shaking his head.

Indeed, Cromwell had not given him the wrong name, but the name of the lady *he* himself had set his sights on, who happened to be the wrong sister as far as Alexander was concerned. Again, he recalled the night of the ball as he had looked across the dance floor at Helen. She had spoken with her sister, Lady Sophie, and Cromwell had misunderstood the direction of Alexander's interest.

Cursing under his breath, Alexander left, wishing he could return to the night of the ball and undo what had been set in motion.

If only.

Chapter Five
TWO LADIES AND ONE LORD

Gritting her teeth, Helen managed to reach the safety and solitude of her chamber before a single tear fell. However, the moment the heavy door closed behind her, sobs tore from her throat. Sobs she tried to muffle by throwing herself on the bed and burying her face in the pillows.

He was courting her sister! How could he?

Again and again, Helen relived the moment she had stepped over the threshold into the drawing room and seen him. Her heart had skipped a beat or two, and her lungs had ceased to draw breath. For a precious moment, she had been lost in his eyes, joy rushing through her body at seeing him again so unexpectedly.

However, that precious moment had been harshly followed by the realisation of the reason that had brought him to their house.

It had not been her.

He had not come to call on her.

But on her sister instead.

How had this happened?

All Helen's hopes and dreams that she had carefully allowed into her heart the night of the ball came crashing down, burying her in a rather nightmarish vision of her future. A vision in which he-Lord

Kensington! -would become Sophie's husband instead. A vision in which she, Helen, would be his sister-in-law. A vision of watching the man she had opened her heart to in her sister's arms.

Closing her eyes, Helen felt her body tremble as her stomach turned and nausea rolled over her in waves. Could this be happening? How? Why?

Had he not kissed her at the ball? Why would he have done so if in truth he had intentions of pursuing her sister?

Groaning, Helen remembered her own words from later that night.

We are both well aware that a kiss is not always born out of deep affection, especially for a man. It might simply have been...the magic of the moment. Nothing more.

Could this be true? Had it simply been the magic of the moment? Could she have been so mistaken?

Again, she heard Sophie's voice whisper of the one man in particular who had caught her interest. I danced with many handsome and gallant gentlemen tonight. However, there was one who...The way he smiled at me made me weak in the knees.

Could it have been Lord Kensington? How had Helen not noticed?

A frown came to her face. Had Sophie not called him a rake? Helen had to admit that that was not the impression she had gotten. Obviously, it was not the only thing she had misunderstood.

Remembering the wistful look in her sister's eyes as she had spoken of *her prince*, Helen felt ill all over again. Sophie cared for him, did she not? Of course, she did. Was there a woman on this planet who could claim to be immune to Lord Kensington's dark and intense gaze? The way he focused all his attention on the woman he was with? The way he made her feel as though she was the only one who mattered?

Certainly not.

In the end, the one clear thought that came from the chaos raging in Helen's heart and mind was that she loved her sister and that Sophie deserved to be happy.

And so, Helen rose from the bed and worked to hide the evidence of her emotional turmoil. Wiping the tears from her eyes, she splashed some cold water on her face, then straightened the bedding to look as though nothing had happened. Then she seated herself in the armchair by the windows and picked up the book she had been reading. However, instead of becoming engrossed in the words on the page before her, her thoughts circled around one thing: Not to stand in Sophie's way to happiness because more than anyone else she deserved to be happy.

Heaving a shuddering sigh, Helen closed her eyes, willing herself to believe the words that echoed in her head like a mantra.

However, by the time the door to her chamber flew open and Sophie strode in, Helen was no closer to believing them in her heart than she had been before. Did that make her an awful sister?

"Why did you run off?" Sophie enquired without preamble. Her watchful eyes travelled over Helen's face, narrowing almost imperceptibly as she sank into the chair opposite Helen.

Swallowing, Helen smiled at her sister. "I felt a bit faint all of a sudden," she replied with a glance at her bed. "I had to lie down for a moment. But it has passed now."

"I see," Sophie mumbled in that way of hers that always meant she saw a great deal more than others wanted her to see. Helen could only hope that her sister's mind was currently not as sharp because it was otherwise engaged, namely with her recent suitor.

"Did you have a pleasant talk with Lord Kensington?" Helen asked, willing her voice not to break as she spoke his name.

Sophie nodded as she sat back, an easy smile coming to her face. "I did indeed. He is a fine gentleman, well-mannered and respectful." She leaned forward and met Helen's gaze. "The kind of man a woman could lose her heart to."

Swallowing, Helen forced her gaze not to drop from her sisters as her heart broke into a million pieces. "That is good news," she breathed, no strength in her voice. "You deserve nothing less."

Sitting back, Sophie watched her for a moment before she said, "He invited me to go horseback riding through Hyde Park tomorrow."

Every word out of her sister's mouth felt like a dagger piercing her heart, and yet, Helen smiled gently, reminding herself that Sophie had done nothing wrong. She had fallen for a wonderful man as he had fallen for her. It was the way of the world, and they were the fortunate ones. "That is wonderful," Helen exclaimed, trying to put a bit more enthusiasm into her voice. "It seems the weather will be perfect for such an outing. I'm certain you will enjoy it greatly."

A hint of disappointment came to Sophie's eyes as Helen spoke, and the spot between her eyes began to crinkle in consternation. "May I ask you a rather personal question?"

Surprised, Helen nearly dropped the book she still held clutched in her hands. Sophie never asked to ask a question. Blessed with a rather forthright manner, she generally got to the point fairly quickly, never once considering whether or not her questions might be considered intrusive. "Certainly," Helen said, nodding, her fingers tensing around the book.

Holding Helen's gaze, Sophie sighed. "Was Lord Kensington the one you met at the Dashwood ball? The one who kissed you?"

Generally, Sophie's rather personal questions had a habit of catching Helen off guard. This time, however, they froze the blood in her veins.

Staring at Sophie, Helen knew that for once in her life she had to lie to her sister. For if she did not, Sophie would sacrifice her own happiness out of loyalty to her, and Helen could not allow that to happen. After all, when two people found each other, they deserved to be together no matter what.

Finding true love was difficult enough in today's world.

And so, Helen planted a soft smile on her face, forced her muscles to relax and said with what she hoped was a touch of incredulity, "Oh, no, it wasn't him. I told you I never got his name."

"I see," Sophie mumbled once more, and Helen prayed that the look on her face was more reassuring than she thought. And if not, if Sophie was not completely convinced, then Helen would simply have to insist again and again until her sister did believe her. This was simply too important a matter. She could not fail. "Then you do not mind that he called on me today?"

Willing her heart to keep beating, Helen shook her head. "No, of course not. I'm happy for you."

"I see." Holding Helen's gaze for a moment longer, Sophie seemed contemplative. Then her demeanour changed, and a large smile transformed her face. "Will you come with me tomorrow?"

"Tomorrow?"

"Yes, will you accompany me tomorrow as a chaperon?" Sophie asked, her eyes sparkling with something Helen could not quite name. "It would put my mind greatly at ease to have you there."

Helen sighed, fighting the urge to close her eyes in despair. "Certainly," she replied, unable to deny her sister such a heartfelt request. After all, if her sister was to marry Lord Kensington, she, Helen, would need to find a way to meet him without breaking down.

It would not be easy and would take practise. And as much as she despised the thought, she might as well start practising tomorrow.

"Wonderful!" Sophie exclaimed. "I'm certain it will be a day worth remembering!"

Helen could only hope that her sister was wrong.

Chapter Six

A DAY WORTH REMEMBERING

Guiding his horse down a winding path in Hyde Park, Alexander could not help but glance over his shoulder. There, not two steps behind him and Lady Sophie rode Helen, her eyes downcast as she tried not to meet his gaze. Did she feel the same despair that had claimed his own heart? Selfishly, Alexander hoped it was true. Or had he been mistaken? Had their encounter at the ball not meant anything to her that she would now encourage her sister to pursue him?

"It is indeed fine weather," Lady Sophie commented, and Alexander forced his attention back to the woman riding beside him. "Sunshine transforms everything, does it not? Even despite the cold, everything seems so warm and pleasant."

"It certainly does," Alexander replied, only half-aware of Lady Sophie's words as his thoughts did not seem willing to abandon their original focus. Again, he glanced over his shoulder...in the very moment Helen lifted her gaze from her hands. Their eyes met, and Alexander could have sworn that the air crackled with the intensity of their shared longing. Her eyes widened as she beheld him, and a becoming blush crept up her cheeks before she forced her eyes back down.

Alexander could have groaned. Was she only avoiding him out of loyalty to her sister? If that was the case, was there anything he could do that would win him not only her heart but also her hand? Or was this a lost cause as her devotion to her sister would never allow Helen to accept him now?

"I find myself wondering," Lady Sophie began, effectively redirecting Alexander's attention to the front, "how Hyde Park received its name." Cocking her head slightly, she glanced at him. "Do you happen to know, my lord?"

Clearing his throat, Alexander tried to focus his thoughts. "I believe it originates from the Manor of Hyde."

"The Manor of Hyde?" Sophie frowned. "I don't believe that name is familiar to me." Amused laughter brightened her face. "I'm afraid this is generally not a topic of interest to me. My sister Helen is much more versed in this area." Half-turning in the saddle, Lady Sophie looked at her sister. "Helen, would you mind joining us?"

Surprised, Alexander allowed his gaze to travel to the woman who had captured his heart so effectively. It seemed equal surprise had widened her eyes and parted her lips as she looked from her sister to him. Then she swallowed and urged her mare closer. "Certainly."

Lady Sophie directed her gelding to the right and closer to him, making room for Helen on her other side. "We were just now speaking of how Hyde Park received its name? I am not wrong to assume that you know the answer, am I?"

Fidgeting with the reins in her hand, Helen turned to him, her gaze meeting his for a mere second before she glanced back at her sister. "I believe it stems from the Manor of Hyde," she all but whispered.

"Lord Kensington said so as well," Sophie continued, seemingly completely oblivious to the strained atmosphere that engulfed her two companions. "Still, I cannot say I've heard of it before."

"Well," Helen began, her gaze barely meeting her sister's. "This area used to belong to Westminster Abbey, providing fire-wood and shelter for the monks."

Alexander nodded, his gaze fixed on Helen. "Indeed, it did. At least throughout the Middle Ages." Unable to remain quiet, Alexander delighted in finding Helen's eyes find his as he spoke.

"Then how did it come to be a park?" Lady Sophie enquired.

Helen licked her lips, her gaze meeting her sister's before returning to him. Alexander's heart danced in his chest. "I believe Henry VIII acquired it in 1535-"

"Thirty-six," Alexander corrected without thinking.

"Yes, indeed," Helen replied, a genuine smile on her face as she looked at him. "In 1536. He used it as a hunting ground, I believe."

"A private hunting ground," Alexander elaborated, delighting in the way the sun made her beautiful features come alive. "It was only opened to the public about a hundred years later."

A grin came to Helen's face and her eyes sparkled with a hint of mischief as she said, "A hundred and one."

Chuckling, Alexander nodded. "Indeed, a hundred and one." For a long moment, their gazes locked as their steeds carried them down a small slope, the rest of the world forgotten. Only the soft nicker of a horse farther off brought them back to the reality they had all but forgotten.

Blinking, Helen's gaze strayed from his. "Did that answer your ques-?" Turning to look at her sister, Helen stopped, pulling up the reins. "Where is-?"

"There," Alexander exclaimed, surprised and yet relieved to find Lady Sophie a good distance behind them, her gaze turned backwards as she lifted her hand in greeting to an approaching rider.

"Who is that?" Helen asked, her eyes narrowed at the blinding sun.

Alexander chuckled. "I believe that is Lord Cromwell." That man seemed to be everywhere, and Alexander could not help but wonder why. It was certainly clear that he had set his sights on Lady Sophie, however, now, it became more and more apparent that Lady Sophie as well was not completely indifferent to the young lord. Was it possible that her regard for him, Alexander, was not as deep as he had feared? Was there still a chance for him to win Helen's hand?

Fighting to suppress the relieved smile that wanted to burst forth, Alexander said, "He called on your sister yesterday. I met him when I left."

Helen's gaze narrowed as she took in his words before her eyes once more dropped from his and a hint of sadness replaced the joy that had been on her features mere moments ago. Had he said something wrong?

Before Alexander could ask, Lady Sophie and Lord Cromwell rejoined them, talking animatedly as they took the lead with Helen and Alexander following behind. Glancing at the woman beside him, Alexander noticed a hint of confusion come to her features every now and then. However, try as he might, he could not return them to the easy conversation they had enjoyed before. Something had changed. If only he knew what!

Chapter Seven
FOR HER SISTER'S SAKE

Seated in the carriage a few nights later, Helen became increasingly aware with each turn of the wheel that her heart seemed to dance in her chest as it had never before. Never had she counted the minutes it took them to reach an event. Never had she longed to enter a ballroom. Never had she found herself hoping for a certain gentleman's presence.

Her pulse thudded in her veins, and Helen could not deny that a certain lightheadedness engulfed her, almost like the haze of a beautiful dream.

A dream that could never come true.

Whenever her glaze fell on her sister seated next to her, Helen felt like crumbling to the floor in misery. Guilt washed over her, and she chided herself for betraying her sister.

Nevertheless, neither her heart not her thoughts would be deterred.

All Helen could see before her mind's eye was Lord Kensington's charming smile and the way his eyes had looked into hers that sunny afternoon a few days ago.

Curse her weak heart!

Once more glancing at her sister, Helen found her chatting

animatedly with their parents. Had Sophie noticed how Helen had drawn the conversation away from her sister and toward herself that day in Hyde Park? Was that why Sophie had barely spoken a word to her about Lord Kensington since that day? Did she feel betrayed after she had given Helen every opportunity to confide her own feelings for him?

For Helen had come to realise that the only reason for Sophie's inquisitive questions that past afternoon had been to ensure that Helen held no regard for Lord Kensington. Kind, sweet Sophie would not have pursued him if she had known that he also held Helen's heart. However, after Helen's insistent denial, she had felt at liberty to pursue the man she had come to care for...only to have her sister betray her by stealing Lord Kensington's attention.

How could Helen not have noticed that Sophie had fallen behind? That she no longer had contributed to their conversation after so self-lessly inviting Helen to join them?

Closing her eyes, Helen could only hope that her sister was not angry with her. That there was still a chance for Helen to make this right. To take a step back and allow her sister to be happy.

As they entered the ballroom, Helen turned her head to find Sophie loop her arm through hers, a joyous smile on her lips. "Do you see him?" she whispered. "Is he here?"

Helen swallowed. "Who?"

Sophie giggled before leaning closer and whispering in Helen's ear, "The man who kissed you, who else? Do you see him anywhere?"

Inhaling a slow breath, Helen did not know what to say. Would the lies never end? Would she now forever be forced to be dishonest with her sister in order to ensure her happiness?

"If you see him, you must point him out to me at once," Sophie insisted as she pulled Helen onward.

"I don't think he will be here. As I said he rarely seems to attend-"

"I know what you said," Sophie objected, shaking her head at Helen. "Have a little faith. From what you said about him, about...your encounter," mischievous delight lit up her sister's eyes, "I cannot believe that he does not wish to see you again. I'm certain he will attend. Mark my words."

Helen sighed, knowing there was no arguing with Sophie once she had set her mind on something.

"There he is!"

"How would you kno-?" Helen began, turning in the direction her sister indicated, only to find herself staring at Lord Kensington. For a moment, all blood drained from her face before she realised that Sophie was simply referring to the man *she* herself had kept an eye out for. "Oh," was all Helen could say as her sister dragged her forward.

As always Sophie had been right. Lord Kensington was in attendance. However, he had come to see Sophie that night, not her.

Striding across the ballroom, Helen noticed Lord Cromwell approaching, and she braced herself for the spectacle of seeing these two gentlemen fight over her sister's attention.

After greetings were exchanged, both men complimented Sophie on the gown she had chosen that night, only belatedly offering compliments to Helen as well.

"Would you care to dance?" Lord Cromwell asked her sister, almost tripping over his tongue as he rushed to procure her hand presumably before Lord Kensington could interfere.

Smiling, Sophie took his hand. "Certainly, my lord."

Helen swallowed as she noticed the slight tension in Lord Kensington's jaw as he forced his gaze from the couple standing up for a country dance. Turning to her, a small smile came to his lips that nearly turned her knees to pudding.

Gritting her teeth, Helen reminded herself that it would do her no good if she were to fall for her potential brother-in-law!

"Would you like to dance?"

For a moment, Helen simply stared at him before she rediscovered her voice. "There is no need to offer simply because-"

"I want to dance with you," he whispered, his gaze intense as it held hers.

For a moment-a weak moment! - Helen allowed herself to believe that he truly did wish to dance with her. Before she knew what was happening, she found herself following him onto the dance floor, his hand wrapped around hers as he guided her feet.

As the dance began, Helen did her best not to notice the warmth in his eyes or the gentle curl to his lips as he looked at her. After all, there was no use living in a fantasy. All it would lead to was heartbreak. No, it was important she did not forget who he came here to see. "My sister looks quite breath-taking tonight, does she not?"

For a moment, Lord Kensington's eyes narrowed as though he was confused. Then his gaze drifted to her sister. "She does look beautiful," he agreed, and despite her best efforts, Helen's heart sank. "And she seems to be enjoying herself greatly."

At his observation, Helen turned her head to see her sister smiling at Lord Cromwell adoringly.

"Her heart does not beat for me," Lord Kensington whispered when the dance brought them back together. His breath brushed over her skin, momentarily distracting her thoughts as her body shivered with his nearness.

Once they were apart again, Helen's mind cleared, urging her to encourage him not to give up lest he break her sister's heart. "You are mistaken, my lord," Helen told him, willing her voice to sound light but determined. "She admires you greatly and might simply be trying to gauge your interest by feigning indifference. I urge you not to give up. There is no finer woman in all of England than my sister."

For a moment, Lord Kensington stared at her as though in disbelief before his features hardened in determination. Helen could only hope that her words had persuaded him not to give up hope.

At least for her sister's sake.

Chapter Eight
A LADY'S PARTICULAR INTEREST

Unable not to, Alexander found himself across the room staring at Helen.

Had she truly meant what she had said? Did she truly want him to pursue her sister? Could she not see that Lady Sophie only had eyes for Cromwell? Or was it her way of refusing him? Could he have been so mistaken about their encounter at the Dashwood ball?

All this time, Alexander had hoped that she had merely tried to discourage him out of loyalty to her sister. But what if he was wrong?

Bowing over Lady Sophie's hand, Cromwell took his leave and, to Alexander's great dismay, came walking across the room straight toward him, an annoyingly amused smile on his face. "Good evening again, Kensington," the man greeted him. "It is quite a marvellous night, is it not?"

Already annoyed, Alexander had to force himself to remain civil. "It would appear so," he grumbled, unable to hide his displeasure.

A low chuckle escaped Cromwell as he came to stand beside Alexander, his arms linked behind his back, his gaze drifting across the dance floor to the two sisters. "You look miserable," he observed dryly. "Did the fair lady refuse your suit?"

Pressing his lips together painfully, Alexander fought the urge to put Cromwell in his place. How dare the man address him so informally! "That is none of your concern," he finally forced out through clenched teeth. In that moment, Alexander did not know what pained him more, Helen's refusal or Cromwell's amusement.

Inhaling deeply, Cromwell turned to him, his face uncharacteristically sober. "Whether you like it or not, *my friend*," Cromwell began, a hint of amusement back in his voice, "I am here to help you."

Caught off guard, Alexander turned to stare at his peer. Indeed, these had been the last words he would have expected to hear from the man. "What is it to you?" His eyes narrowed. "What is your agenda?"

Cromwell chuckled, "To win Lady Sophie's hand." As he spoke, all humour left his face, and Alexander stared in amazement at a man very much in love.

A man he knew only too well.

A man like himself.

Still, despite what his eyes saw, Alexander did not dare trust Cromwell so easily. "Then go charm the lady," he said flatly. "Why would my...dealings be any concern of yours?"

Sighing rather exasperatedly, Cromwell rolled his eyes. "Fine, let's be frank. Lady Sophie *instructed* me to speak to you and urge you not to give up on her sister."

Alexander's eyes bulged. "Why would she do that?" His frown deepened. "Why would you?"

His forehead creased with a deep frown, Cromwell shook his head at Alexander. "Kensington, I must say on occasion you're a bit daft. Lady Helen is her sister, and she wants to see her happy. I thought as a man with two sisters of his own you'd be aware of the strong bond that apparently exists between two of their kind."

Alexander swallowed, his ears ringing with the words Cromwell threw at him.

Taking a step closer, Cromwell leaned forward, his gaze holding Alexander's imploringly. "She urges you not to give up," he repeated. "Do not let Lady Helen discourage you from pursuing her."

Shaking his head, Alexander scoffed. "What a coincidence? Only moments ago, Lady Helen urged *me* not to give up on pursuing her sister. I would think such a statement makes the lady's feelings on the matter overwhelmingly clear."

"Does it?" Cromwell dared him, brows rising into arches. "Listen, Kensington, do what you want, but be careful not to misread a lady's heart."

"What would you know of this?"

"Only what her sister told me," Cromwell replied. "Apparently, Lady Helen is only discouraging you out of respect for her sister, believing her in love with you." A hint of a snarl came to Cromwell's face. "Quite obviously, she does not see that Lady Sophie has no particular interest in you, at least not beyond a brother-in-law."

Alexander inhaled a slow breath. Could Cromwell be correct? Had he truly spoken to Lady Sophie? Or was this some elaborate game? Still, despite the hint of humour that lingered on his face, the man seemed to be speaking in earnest. Did Alexander dare believe him?

Turning his gaze from Cromwell, Alexander looked across the dance floor toward the two sisters. As though Helen could feel him looking, her own eyes turned from her sister and met his. In that instant, it was as though a shock wave went through them, and he felt her gaze all the way to his bones. She, too, appeared affect as her cheeks flushed a becoming red, and her eyes quickly darted to the floor before returning to meet his.

"I would say it's rather obvious," Cromwell chuckled beside him. "What I can't figure out is why the two of you do not see it?"

Reluctantly dropping his gaze from Helen's, Alexander looked at Cromwell, his eyes narrowing as he tried to understand the man. "Why would any of this matter to you?"

Cromwell shrugged, his eyes darting back across the dance floor, presumably to gaze upon Lady Sophie. "I want her," he finally said without preamble before his eyes returned to meet Alexander's, "and I want her to be happy. And if her sister's happiness is what it takes, then I will do everything within my power to ensure it."

Alexander inhaled a slow breath, surprised to have misjudged Cromwell so. Or had he undergone a change since he had laid eyes on Lady Sophie? Could love truly change a man so?

"What will you do?" Cromwell asked, tension resting on his face.

Surprised, Alexander realised that he not only held his own happiness in his hands, but Cromwell's as well. "I do not know," he finally said. "I wish I did."

Again, his gaze returned to Helen, drifting over her as she spoke to her sister, then turned to her father, laughing at something he had said. Could they be right? Alexander wondered. Certainly, he would agree that Lady Sophie knew her sister best. But was her judgement truly unimpaired? Or did her own hopes and dreams cloud her eyes?

If only he knew.

Chapter Nine
TO BE SPOKEN OF

Once again, after they had returned late from that night's ball, Helen heard Sophie's footsteps approaching her door. Moments later, it was pushed open, and her sister marched in, rather unceremoniously climbing into Helen's bed.

In the dim light from the single candle burning on Helen's bedside table, she found her sister's eyes meeting hers, a strange spark in them that Helen could not quite explain.

"May I ask you a question?" Sophie began, and once again, Helen felt the little hairs on the back of her neck rise.

"If you wish."

Crossing her arms in front of her chest, Sophie held her gaze, her own narrowing in challenge. "Why do you keep pretending that you're not in love with Lord Kensington?"

As though the world had just dropped off its axis, Helen's eyes and mouth dropped unbecomingly open as she stared at her sister. Her pulse raced, and her heart twisted at the thought of Sophie's anger and disappointment. Had she truly been that transparent?

Oh, what would she do now? Would Sophie ever forgive her? "I'm not," Helen stammered, at a loss about what else to say. "I don't know... what...what gave you that idea. It's...it's preposterous."

Averting her gaze, Helen busied her hands smoothing down the blanket.

To Helen's utter surprise, Sophie laughed. "You've always been a bad liar, dear sister, and I mean that as a compliment. Just think if you were actually good at lying, I might never have seen the truth and might not have been able to prevent you from making a big mistake."

Confused, Helen lifted her gaze to Sophie's. "What are you speaking of? What mistake?"

Exhaling loudly, Sophie shook her head. "Lord Kensington is the man who kissed you at the Dashwood ball, isn't he?"

Helen tried her best to swallow the lump in her throat, but it would not move.

"Don't deny it! It is written all over your face." Sighing, Sophie's features softened, and she reached out to place a gentle hand on Helen's arm. "Why do you refuse him?"

Again, Helen's eyes opened wide. "I am not. He...he doesn't want me. He wants you."

Throwing back her head, Sophie laughed, and for a good minute, Helen stared at her in utter shock. "That is ludicrous!" Sophie finally replied once she had caught her breath.

"But...but he came to call on you," Helen said feebly as her mind raced and her heart ached.

Sophie sobered. "I'm certain it was a mistake. Perhaps he did not dare call on you, fearing you would refuse him. Perhaps he wanted to speak to me...about you."

"Did he?" Helen asked, afraid of the sliver of hope that was beginning to fight its way to the surface.

"He spoke *of* you," Sophie whispered, a delighted gleam in her dark eyes. "He told me that you *enlightened* him, that you spoke to him of artefacts."

Helen's shoulders slumped. "We merely talked."

"And kissed," Sophie added, a wicked smile on her face.

Helen felt herself blush, realising how much she wanted her sister's words to be true, and yet, she did not dare believe them. "That does not matter," Helen insisted. "He came to call on you. He invited you to Hyde Park."

Sophie laughed, "Well, in all honesty, I *made* him extend that invitation. I didn't leave him much choice, not if he wanted to remain the honourable gentleman he is."

Helen frowned. "Why? If you do not care for him, why on earth would you urge him to invite you?"

"So, *you* could see him again," Sophie explained. "After you burst into the room, it became quite clear that he had been the one to kiss you at the ball, and what became even clearer was that you two care for each other."

Again, Helen felt heat rush to her cheeks. Her heart warmed at her sister's kind words as well as the thought that Lord Kensington might truly hold a deeper regard for her.

"I never cared for him," Sophie continued, her hand gently squeezing Helen's. "I promise you. And I know that you only pretended not to care for him out of respect for me." Hugging her tightly, Sophie sighed. "I love you for your loyalty, dear sister, but there is no need for it here." Sitting back, Sophie met Helen's eyes. "I've lost my heart-I admit that freely-but not to Lord Kensington."

Blinking back tears, Helen smiled. "Lord Cromwell?" Sophie nodded. "I thought you only meant to test Lord Kensington's regard. I thought you wished to see if he would fight for you."

Sophie smiled, brushing a tear from Helen's cheek. "Well, he didn't, and I never wanted him to, of that you can be certain. But," Sophie lifted a finger as though in warning, "when he finds the courage to fight for you, you must promise me that you'll let him win your heart. Don't hide yourself away from the world. As wonderful as your books are, they cannot compare to true love. Please, Helen, promise me."

"I promise," Helen whispered, staring into her sister's kind face.

Perhaps, just perhaps, their father had been right in choosing their names. After all, if her sister was right-and Helen prayed with all her heart that she was-then Sophie possessed a rare talent for seeing the truth.

And what greater wisdom was there in life than seeing what was true.

Chapter Ten

TO CALL ON A LADY YET AGAIN

Hope and doubt warred within Alexander as he found himself once more awaiting Lady Sophie in her family's drawing room. Why he did not call on Helen, he could not say. Still, after what Cromwell had told him at the ball, Lady Sophie seemed to be the one to speak to.

"Good day, Lord Kensington," she greeted him a few minutes later, her wide green eyes sweeping over his face. "I must admit I am once more surprised that you would call on me."

Alexander swallowed, suddenly at a loss as to what to say. His heart knew very well what he wanted to know. However, his mind could not seem to conjure the necessary words. Belatedly, he mumbled a greeting and then took a seat at Lady Sophie's invitation, relieved to see that today there was no maid chaperoning their meeting. It would be easier to speak without watchful eyes trained on him.

"What brings you here on this fine day, my lord?" Lady Sophie asked, the hint of an amused smile curling her lips. Could she see his turmoil? His indecision? His doubt?

"I came to take my leave." Frowning, Alexander stopped. Had he? "I plan to take a journey to the continent...to meet a friend, and I expect to be gone for a while." Gritting his teeth, Alexander wondered where these words had come from.

Lady Sophie's gaze narrowed. "I see," she mumbled, her piercing green eyes holding his in frank perusal. "May I ask you a fairly personal question, my lord?"

Swallowing, Alexander managed a nod as his thoughts strayed to Helen...somewhere in this house. Where was she? What was she doing? Did she know that he was here? Did she care?

"In all honesty, my lord," Lady Sophie began, "to me, it seems as though you're running away." Tension gripped Alexander's shoulders. "And so, I ask you openly, are you?"

Gritting his teeth, Alexander swallowed. "I'm afraid I do not know what you speak of, my lady?"

A large smile spread over her face before she shook her head, a light chuckle escaping her lips. "You are more alike than you know," she whispered as though to herself before her green gaze returned to hold his. "You care for my sister," she said without preamble.

As though struck, Alexander shot to his feet.

A triumphant gleam came to Lady Sophie's eyes as she rose as well, taking a measured step toward him. "I would even go as far as saying that you're in love with her."

Again, Alexander swallowed. "What gave you that impression?" he croaked, finally doubting the wisdom in coming here today.

"You kissed her, did you not?"

A jolt went through Alexander at her frank words, and he stared at her in shock, aware of her watchful eyes taking in every subtle nuance of his reaction. "I did," he admitted, wondering what she would say next.

"Why?"

"Why?" Alexander repeated rather dumbfounded.

"Yes, why?" Approaching, Lady Sophie watched him, a hint of a challenge in her eyes. "Were you merely looking to...amuse yourself? Or-?"

"Never!" Alexander growled, anger clearing his head at her suggestion that he had dishonourable intentions toward her sister.

A small smile curled up her lips. "Good," she whispered as though pleased to see him react thus. "Then why?" she dared him.

Torn between speaking the truth as well as admitting his feelings not only to himself but to the world in general and guarding his heart as well as his pride, Alexander held her gaze, the muscles in his jaw flexing with the indecision that warred within him.

Lady Sophie's features softened as she took in his turmoil. "Do you love her?" she whispered, and for once there was no challenge in her gaze, merely the desire to know the truth.

Alexander sighed. "I do," he finally admitted, and as though a heavy weight had been lifted off his heart, it grew lighter with each breath he took. "She's...I've never met a woman like her."

Lady Sophie smiled. "I'm pleased to hear that. However, to the one person who matters, you have not said a word, have you?"

Alexander felt his muscles tense. "Do you think...? Do you believe she could...truly come to care for me?" For a moment, his gaze drifted from hers before he forced himself to meet her eyes once again.

A gentle smile played on her lips as she stepped forward and placed her hand on his cheek. "Dear Brother, I know that love makes one blind, and, therefore, I will not hold it against you that you do not see...that she already does. She is equally afraid to admit her feelings, fearing they will not be returned."

A gust of air rushed from Alexander's lungs, and he could not help the smile that spread over his face. "She does?"

Lady Sophie nodded. "She does." Dropping her hand, she took a step back, her watchful eyes intent on his. "Now, I suggest you speak to her before you do anything rash. Before you do something you will come to regret for the rest of your life." She sighed. "The choice is yours. Do you wish to leave? Or do you wish for me to fetch my sister?"

Inhaling a slow breath, Alexander smiled. "I will not leave without speaking to her."

"Good." Relief played in Lady Sophie's eyes as she turned toward the door. However, before she left, she glanced over her shoulder, her eyes meeting his once more. "I believe I shall like having you for a brother."

Then she was gone, and Alexander found himself staring at the closed door, praying that Lady Sophie's words would live up to her name.

Chapter Eleven
DEAR, WISE SOPHIE

Ever since Sophie had been called downstairs to receive Lord Kensington, Helen had been pacing the length of her room, her thoughts a chaotic mess.

Why had he come? She longed to know, wringing her hands nervously. Why had he called on her sister again? Why had he not called on her instead? After all, if Sophie were right that he cared for her, Helen, would he not have come to call on her instead of her sister?

Closing her eyes and stilling her feet, Helen inhaled a deep breath, feeling her heart flutter in her chest. What was she to do?

Helen felt her sister's presence more than she heard the door to her chamber opening. "Yes, I can see that you do not care for him at all, dear sister!" Sophie teased, a large smile on her face as she regarded Helen with amusement.

Helen swallowed. "I would ask you not to tease me," she said, sinking into her favourite armchair and folding her hands in her lap. "Especially not today, not when his actions just proved you wrong."

Closing the door, Sophie strolled into the room, the look on her face one of complete and utter delight. "Why would you assume I have been proved wrong?"

Shaking her head, Helen sighed. "He is here, is he not? He came to call on you...again." Huffing under her breath, Helen did her best to remind herself that none of this was her sister's fault. She ought not to blame Sophie for being the preferred sister.

Laughing, Sophie came to sit by Helen's feet and drew her sister's hands into her own. "My dear, Helen, I assure you I was not proven wrong. Quite the opposite. He never wanted me, not for a single moment. He came here because he loves *you*."

Staring at her sister, Helen tried to absorb the words she had just heard. "But...but...then why did he call on you?" Gritting her teeth, Helen fought down the sliver of treacherous hope that always seemed to be lurking nearby, waiting for a moment of weakness in order to overpower her.

A rather indulgent smile came to Sophie's face. "Because he fears you do not return his affections."

"How can you be certain?" Helen gasped almost breathless as her heart pounded in her chest and her head grew dizzy.

"He told me so," Sophie replied. "It is fairly obvious, and Lord Cromwell agreed with my assessment days ago."

Helen's eyes flew open. "You spoke to Lord Cromwell about this? How could you?"

"I needed an ally in this, didn't I?" Sophie exclaimed, a hint of a challenge in her green eyes. "Neither you nor Lord Kensington were any help in the matter. You didn't truly expect me to do all of the matchmaking myself, did you?" A teasing grin drew up the corners of Sophie's lips.

Helen frowned. "Why would he help you? Why would he care if...?" Her voice trailed off as she took in the deep smile and glowing eyes gracing her sister's face. "He loves you," Helen whispered in awe. "He was the one who made you feel weak in the knees, wasn't he?"

Sophie nodded. "He may be a rake, but he is my rake."

"Are you not concerned that-?"

Smiling, Sophie shook her head vehemently. "He's proved himself to me. He was there when I needed him, and he asked for nothing in return. He urged Lord Kensington not to give up. He did that for me because my happiness would not be complete without yours, dear sister."

Looking into her sister's eyes, Helen could not help but recognise herself in the woman before her. Not that she had the same courage and faith as her little sister, but they both had lost their hearts to another. Helen was certain that this would strengthen the bond between them forever.

"Go downstairs," Sophie urged, pulling Helen to her feet, "and be honest. That man loves you, and he has the same doubts and fears that give you pause as well."

Tears came to Helen's eyes as her emotions surged to the surface threatening to overwhelm her. Never in her life had she felt so completely blessed than in this moment. Hugging her beloved sister tightly, she closed her eyes, savouring the feeling of being so completely loved that it almost hurt.

"Go to him. I've made certain that you can speak alone," Sophie urged, tears clinging to her lashes. "Don't make him wait. He's most likely pacing the drawing room like a caged animal."

Unable to suppress a chuckle, Helen nodded. "Thank you...for everything."

"What are sisters for?" Sophie asked as she pushed Helen gently out the door. "Now, don't delay. Go!"

Taking a deep breath, Helen hurried down the hallway and then descended the stairs to the ground floor, her hands trembling as she tried to smooth down her skirts-anything to keep her busy. The lump still hung in her throat, and she blinked her eyes fiercely to dispel the last tears. Then she tugged a stray curl behind her ear, brushed the wetness off her cheeks and took another deep breath as she came to stand outside the drawing room.

Courage, she whispered to herself before she opened the door and stepped over the threshold.

The moment her eyes found his, Helen knew that Sophie had been right.

Dear, wise Sophie.

Love shone in his gaze as clearly as the bright sun on a cold wintry day, and Helen wondered how she could have missed it before. Had he always looked at her thus? Had she truly been blinded by her fear to break her sister's heart? To have her own broken as well?

Smiling, Helen stepped toward him, knowing that none of that mattered now. It was the past, and she would not dwell on it any longer. Joy flooded her heart, and she blinked her eyes fiercely to keep at bay fresh tears.

Tears of happiness.

Utter and complete happiness.

Chapter Twelve
UTTER HAPPINESS

ears! Alexander's mind screamed with an almost deafening roar. *She's crying! Why was she crying?*

His heart tightened in his chest, and he had to force air down into his lungs as his chest seemed unable to expand. His eyes narrowed as they trailed a tear down her cheek until it touched the corner of her mouth. There, it lingered, and to his utter astonishment, Alexander noted the slight upward curve of her lips. Was she smiling?

Blinking his eyes, he tried to focus his gaze...as well as his thoughts.

Indeed, a gentle smile played on her soft lips.

"Is something wrong?" Alexander finally asked, deciding that knowing could not be worse than not knowing. "Did something happen?"

At his question, her smile deepened, and her eyes seemed to glow like emeralds. "I'm fine," she breathed, her voice soft but resolved. "Nothing is wrong. On the contrary, I've been told something...rather pleasant." Colour rose to her cheeks as she bit her lower lip shyly.

Alexander's heart stopped. "What did you hear?" he croaked, his thoughts immediately drifting to the admission he had made to Helen's sister not long ago.

Lifting her chin, she met his gaze. "That you care for me."

His eyes held hers, and Alexander could not help but admire the strength with which she addressed him. Although there was a slight tremble in her hands as they held one another tightly, she stood tall, her eyes urging him to answer her silent question.

"I've heard something pleasant as well," Alexander replied as he slowly reached for her hands. When his fingers brushed hers, she flinched and drew in a sharp breath. Her hands, however, opened to his without hesitation, and before he knew it, they were resting snugly inside his own...as though they belonged there and always had. "I've never met a woman like you," Alexander whispered, his gaze trained on hers, "but I always hoped I would. The night we met, I...it was so unexpected. I felt like a fool for allowing you to leave without even asking your name. If I only had," he shook his head, a disbelieving smile coming to his face, "none of this...this confusion, this misunderstanding would have happened."

Smiling, she took a step closer, her eyes darting to their joined hands before her gaze sought his once more. "When you came to call on my sister that day-"

"I came to see *you*," Alexander hastened to explain. "That night when you rushed back to the ballroom, I followed you. But then I saw you speaking to your sister-as I now know-and I stood back." Closing his eyes, Alexander shook his head at the memory. It seemed like ages had passed since then. "Cromwell approached, his eyes travelling to you as well, and I-"

"But they didn't, did they?" Helen interrupted, a sweet smile on her lips as she looked up at him. "He was looking at my sister."

Alexander chuckled, "I know that now, but then...then all I could think of was that he would steal you away."

A heart-breaking smile lit up Helen's beautiful face, and her hands clung to him more tightly. "You truly thought so?"

Alexander nodded. "How could I not? Within moments you had bewitched me, and then when he spoke of a rare woman, I never once thought to question to whom he was referring. He said your name, and I...I simply...I saw only you." He swallowed. "I thought your name was Sophie, and so I came to call on you as soon as I could muster the courage to do so." Pulling her closer, he allowed all fear to fall from him and spoke with his heart. "When your sister entered instead of you, I was stumped. But then when I saw you and realised the mistake I had made, I was devastated because I felt certain I had lost you for good." He inhaled a deep breath. "I could have kicked myself for being such a fool, and I don't ever want to feel like that again. I don't ever want to have regrets like these again."

A slight frown came to her face, but her eyes brightened with expectation. "What are you saying?"

Forcing himself to draw in another breath of air lest he drop dead at her feet, Alexander pulled her into his arms. His smile deepened when she came to him without even the slightest hint of uncertainty in her green eyes. "I love you," he whispered, delighting in the glow that came to her beautiful face. "Please do me the honour of accepting my hand."

At his request, the air rushed from her lungs, and her eyes widened in a most becoming way.

"Please," Alexander whispered. "I don't ever want to spend another day without you ever again, and I most certainly don't want to risk anyone stealing you away." His hands tightened on her back. "You're mine. Mine forever."

Joy gave colour to her cheeks as she smiled up at him, her eyes misting with new tears. And finally, finally, Alexander understood the emotions that held her heart. "Yes," she breathed as her smile widened as though she could not contain her joy.

Releasing the breath he had been holding, Alexander could have wept with joy as well. Instead, he swept her into his arms and twirled her in a tight circle, their shared laughter echoing through the room. All tension fell from him, and the moment, he set her back on his feet, his mouth claimed hers in a kiss that tied them to one another for all eternity.

Her hands came to rest on the back of his neck, and he could feel the tips of her fingers trail over his skin, sending shivers up and down his back. Lost in the moment and the hope for a future with her by his side, Alexander could have continued to kiss her forever.

Still, they would have to make it official, and it would not serve him if he forgot himself now. Loosening his hold on her, Alexander looked deep into her eyes, knowing how fortunate he was that a minor misunderstanding had not led to a life full of regret and sorrow.

Alexander whispered a silent thank-you to Helen's determined and meddlesome sister, for without her help, he doubted that he would now be the happiest man alive.

"We will be utterly happy, won't we?" she whispered, her eyes aglow with love and hope as he held her in his arms.

"I will make certain of that," Alexander vowed, "if it's the last thing I do."

Epilogue

Westmore Manor, 1754

Three Years Later

Looping her arm through her sister's, Helen guided them down the small slope and into the gardens of Westmore Manor, her husband's ducal home and the place where they had become a family. The sun shone brightly, and birds chirped all around the garden, welcoming another beautiful summer's day.

"I'm so glad you could come," Helen whispered, holding tightly to her sister. "I've missed you terribly."

A radiant smile lit up Sophie's face. "I've missed you as well. Even after all this time, it still feels strange not to live in the same house anymore."

Helen nodded in agreement. "How long can you stay?" she asked, hope evident in her voice.

Sophie grinned. "Pierce said that decision was up to me."

Laughing, Helen shook her head, wondering if her brother-in-law had lost his mind. "Does he know that he will probably never see his home again?"

Sophie wiggled her brows mischievously. Then she sighed, and the look on her face became one of utter adoration. "I think he does," she said wistfully as her gaze travelled over the grounds to where their husbands raced around in the shadow of a large oak, their two-year-old sons riding on their shoulders. "He does it for me." Her gaze returned to Helen, and she gently squeezed her hands. "Ever since we first met, he's known that we, my dearest sister, are two halves of a whole. One cannot exist without the other, and he would never ask me to."

Brushing a stray tear from her sister's cheek, Helen smiled. "He truly loves you, doesn't he?"

Sophie laughed, dabbing at her eyes. "To his utter surprise, yes. Sometimes, I catch him staring at me, shaking his head as though he still cannot believe it to be true." Grinning, she sighed, her gaze returning to her husband and son. "I never thought I'd ever be this happy."

Helen laughed, "Truly? And here I thought you were the wise one."

"Well, I do what I must, and I speak my mind," Sophie replied with a chuckle, "but I know no more than any one of us." Then she shrugged, a twinkle coming to her eyes. "Perhaps I hide it better."

Arm in arm, they proceeded down the small slope toward the large oak tree, and Helen realised how much she had missed Sophie and her family. "Promise me we will never be apart for this long again."

Squeezing her arm, Sophie nodded. "I promise. Never again."

"Faster, Papa! Faster!" Helen's two-year-old son George yelled as he patted his father's head vigorously, urging him on. In turn, Alexander seemed to be panting under his breath, his face growing redder by the second as he raced around with his son on his shoulders. From the looks of it, Pierce fared no better.

Laughing, Helen and Sophie stood arm in arm, watching in delight as their families grew closer with each shared moment. Although life had kept them apart a few months too long, Helen vowed that she would make an extra effort from now on to ensure that they would not drift apart again. Always had she walked through life arm in arm with her sister whenever possible. They had even shared the same wedding day, and as though fate wished to applaud them, their two sons had been born exactly nine months later...on the same day.

Helen could only hope that fate would continue to smile on them and always allow them to share in each other's lives, for better or for worse.

Preferably for the better.

Stopping in front of her, Alexander drew their little boy from his shoulders, sweat running down his temples as he held the squirming child. "Next time, I'll ride on your shoulders," he promised, a wide grin on his face as he sat his son on the ground. Then he leaned over, bracing his hands on his knees and drew in one breath after another.

Helen laughed, placing a gentle hand on her husband's shoulder as she met her sister's eyes. "It would seem the horses are exhausted," she teased, seeing the same mischievous sparkle in Sophie's gaze as she tended to Pierce. "Perhaps they need a little water and some hay."

Little George jumped to his feet, clearly taken with the suggestion, and grabbed a hold of his father's necktie. "Come, horsey! To the stables."

Groaning, Alexander swept his son into his arms and tickled him ferociously until tears of laughter streamed down George's little face. Then he set him down once more. "Go play with your cousin," he instructed, giving him a slight pat on the behind, "before the horsey nips you."

Squealing with delight, George raced off toward Henry, and before long the two boys were engrossed in yet another game.

"You," Alexander said, his voice deep as he turned to Helen. His gaze fixed on hers, he approached with almost menacing steps, the corners of his mouth twitching with humour. "I thought you were on my side," he accused as Helen backed away laughing.

"A mother is always on her child's side, did you not know?" she teased, catching a glimpse of her brother-in-law as he swept a laughing Sophie into his arms.

"I suspected," Alexander said sheepishly before he lunged forward.

Surprised, Helen screamed when his hand closed around her arm, tugging her forward and sweeping her into his embrace. Laughing, she clung to him as he swung her in a circle.

Breathing hard, her husband set her down, his arms holding her close, his eyes shining brightly as he looked down at her. "Is there still room in your heart for me?"

Smiling, Helen snuggled closer. "Always," she whispered, lifting her face to his. "Always and forever."

Returning her smile, Alexander brushed his knuckles along the line of her jaw, his gaze holding hers with an intensity as though he had forgotten all the world around them. "You're mine," he whispered as he had so long ago before his lips claimed hers, binding her to him yet again.

Forever.

Westmore Manor, 1779

25 Years Later

"Graham is a sweet one," Sophie observed as she and Helen walked down the small slope into the gardens. It was their path, one they always walked when her sister's family came to visit. A path they walked arm in arm, sharing what they had missed in each other's lives. It had always been so, and it always would be. "Look, how he tends to Edmond."

Helen smiled, her eyes resting on her five-year-old grandson. "He always seems to have an eye on him like an older brother."

Sophie nodded, glancing up at the terrace where their grown sons, George and Henry, stood with their fathers, their faces bright and full of joy at this family reunion. Laughter drifted to their ears before the echo of little feet drew their attention.

Barely one-year-old Leonora, Sophie's granddaughter and Edmond's little sister, came racing across the terrace, directing her little feet toward the slope that led down to where her brother and cousin where playing in the shade of the old oak. "Emo!" she called, her young mouth trying its best to pronounce her brother's name.

"She is a wild one," Helen observed, smiling at the golden-haired child as she raced as fast as her little feet could carry her. "Not one for patience."

Sophie laughed. "Not at all. Nothing can stop her. No matter what you say or how many obstacles you throw in her path, she will keep going." Shaking her head in disbelief, Sophie sighed. "You know, when she pulled herself up for the first time at barely seven-month-old, I couldn't believe it. And when she then took her first step not a minute later, I knew we were all in trouble."

"She's a handful," Helen replied, watching Leonora struggle to keep her balance as the ground sloped down. "She'll need someone to look out for her."

"As annoyed as he often acts with her, Edmond still adores her," Sophie said proudly, "and Graham does as well. I think she is fortunate to have them."

Helen nodded, sucking in a sharp breath when Leonora suddenly lost her balance and tipped forward, rolling down the remainder of the small slope.

At the little girl's exclamation of surprise-rather than pain!-time seemed to stop as conversations ceased and all eyes turned to Leonora landing in a heap in the grass.

Still, it was little Graham who was the first to shake off the shock. Sprinting to her side, he held out his hand to her, pulling her back onto her feet. Gently, he brushed a blond curl from her face as she in turn brushed her dirt-stained hands on her crisp pale blue dress.

A moment later, laughter bubbled from her mouth, and Graham smiled as he took her hand and they walked back to where Edmond stood waiting.

"There is nothing more important than family," Helen whispered, lost in the scene before her. Always had she hoped for them to remain close, to see their children and now grandchildren grow up together. It was a great comfort to her to know that they had each other. No matter what might happen in the future, they would walk their path together.

Just like her and Sophie.

Family.

Forever.

THE END

This was the prequel to the *Love's Second Chance Series*. If you enjoyed it, read on about how Graham (Alexander and Helen's grandson) and Edmond (Pierce and Sophie's grandson) find their match in *Forgotten & Remembered - The Duke's Late Wife* as well as *Cursed & Cherished - The Duke's Wilful Wife*.

Beyond those two, many more love stories await.

Have you read all 8 books of the **Love's Second Chance Series: Tales of Lords & Ladies?**

Are you ready to get started with the second part of the *Love's Second Chance Series?*

Do you remember Ellie from book 1, *Forgotten & Remembered?*

She gets her own story in the very first installment of the **Love's Second Chance Series: Tales of Damsels & Knights**!

After suffering a tragedy, she suddenly finds herself married to Frederick, a man she's loved almost all her life. Will Ellie be able to claim his heart?

Read a Sneak-Peek

Despised & Desired
The Marquess' Passionate Wife
(#1 Tales of Damsels & Knights)

Prologue

England 1794 (or a variation thereof)

Beads of sweat formed on Ellie's brow and ran down her temples. Trying to shield her face from the scorching sun, she pulled her bonnet deeper into her face. Ellie knew she ought not to be here, and yet, she could not help herself.

The rising heat of this year's unusually hot summer had her escape the earl's garden party in search of a little refreshment.

Excitement had seized her when she had heard other children whisper about the small brook that snaked its way through the forest to the south of the manor. However, uncertain whether or not to dare go against her mother's rather stern instructions of proper conduct, Ellie had waited until the very last moment before she was sure she would melt away. Only then had she dared sneak away.

Now, following in its general direction, Ellie soon heard the soft babbling of the small brook as it fought the sun for its continued existence.

Stepping over large boulders and wading through a sea of long-stemmed grass, Ellie glimpsed the brook's shiny surface, glistening in the sun like an oasis in a desert. Hurrying her step, she hastened toward it at the very moment it seemed to beckon her closer.

A smile spread over her face as she beheld the cool water before her feet. Kneeling down, Ellie reached out a hand, and a soft moan escaped her lips when the fresh water touched her heated skin. For a moment, she closed her eyes, feeling a slight chill run from her submerged hand up her arm. It felt wonderful!

Opening her eyes, Ellie scanned her surroundings and found a cluster of trees a little farther down the stream providing ample shade. Reluctantly withdrawing her hand from the cooling brook, she strode through the grass and then sank down under the trees' large canopy. She removed her bonnet and leaned forward, hand searching for the refreshing wet. Collecting a little water in her cupped hand, she brushed it across her arms, enjoying the tingle that ran through her. And yet, it wasn't enough.

Not nearly enough.

Eyeing her shoes and stockinged feet with a hint of disgust, Ellie took a deep breath. She really ought not to. Even at twelve years old, Elsbeth Munsford was very much aware that a lady ought not to remove her clothing in public.

Glancing around, Ellie frowned. *What public?*

A mischievous smile spread over her face as her nimble fingers worked to loosen her shoes. When they came off, her stockings quickly followed, and Ellie delighted at the feeling of soft grass under her bare feet. Then she glanced at the water and wiggled her toes.

Taking a deep breath, she pushed all thoughts of her mother away and rose to her feet. After making sure that she was, indeed, alone, Ellie slowly pulled up the hem of her dress, revealing her ankles. Grinning from ear to ear, she bit her lower lip in excitement and then stepped toward the brook.

As the cooling water rushed over her skin, Ellie sighed with delight, wiggling her toes and digging them into the muddy stream bed. For a moment, she closed her eyes, savouring the moment until she realised it still wasn't enough.

The coolness barely spread to her knees, let alone chase away the beads of sweat still popping up on her forehead.

Lifting up her skirts to just above her knees, Ellie revealed a small birthmark that resembled a bird taking flight. Although her mother had always considered it an oddity, relieved it was in a place covered by clothes, Ellie had always felt special because of it, wishing that she, too, could simply spread her wings and fly.

Sighing, Ellie waded deeper into the stream. When the water swirled around her calves, she finally felt its cooling effect spread into every part of her body. Welcoming the slight chill chasing away the hot air resting on her skin, Ellie once more closed her eyes.

Lost in a moment of pure pleasure, Ellie did not hear them coming.

Only when they broke through the underbrush, their boots snapping dry twigs as they went, did Ellie's eyes snap open.

Instantly, shock froze her limbs, and she stared at the three young men standing but a few feet from the water's edge.

In that moment, Ellie was too stunned to observe anything else but the cold that slowly spread through her body, bringing with it an old fear. *What would her mother say?*

Then, she swallowed, and her eyes travelled from the tall, dark-haired youth, who-as her mother had informed her-went by the name of Frederick Lancaster, second son to the Marquess of Elmridge, to the two others standing to his left and right, Oliver Cornell and Kenneth Moreton. While Frederick bore an expression that did not betray his thoughts, his friends looked rather surprised to find her in the stream, the corners of their mouths slowly drawing up into a smile, clearly showing their amusement.

Tears began to form in Ellie's eyes as she slowly backed away toward the other side of the brook.

As though in trance, their eyes followed her until Frederick turned to his friends. "Go back," he ordered them. "Speak of this to no one."

For a second, Oliver seemed ready to argue, but Kenneth grabbed his arm and pulled him back through the underbrush.

Frederick, however, remained behind.

Crossing the stream in a shallower spot, he came toward her, his eyes never leaving hers. When he reached her side, he held out a hand, offering to help her out of the stream.

Uncertain what to do, Ellie looked from his hand to his face.

"Do not be afraid," he spoke. "I mean you no harm."

His dark blue eyes shone as clear as the water still swirling around her legs, and her heart beat slowed. Swallowing, Ellie took his hand, surprised at how hot his skin felt compared to her own, which at this point was rather chilled. A shiver went through her, and he pulled her out of the water.

He smiled at her. "You should put your shoes back on."

Ellie blushed and then hurried back to the shady spot where she had left them. Sitting down, she noted that he stood with his back to her, giving her privacy, and she quickly pulled her stockings over her legs and slipped on her shoes.

Then she stood up, not knowing what to say.

"Are you properly attired?" he asked.

"Yes," Ellie breathed, wondering if he judged her as she knew her mother would as soon as she learnt of this.

He turned around then, a friendly smile on his face. "Allow me to escort you back."

Ellie took a deep breath before closing her eyes for a brief moment. When she opened them again, he stood before her, and she shrank back.

Seeing the fear on her face, he instantly retreated a step. "I apologise. I didn't mean to startle you, but you seemed troubled. Are you injured?"

Ellie shook her head. "Please leave," she whispered, her voice pleading.

He frowned at her. "I cannot leave you alone. Who knows who else might be in these woods?"

Never having contemplated the possibility that a threat might be looming near, Ellie glanced at the tree line in his back. Was he right? Was there danger out there?

"If you are worried about being seen with me," he said, trying to catch her eyes, "I assure you I have no intention of compromising you in any way. I merely suggest that I escort you as far as the gardens. From there, you can make your way back on your own. I will stay back and assure that no harm comes to you." His deep blue eyes looked into hers, and he spoke with a sincerity beyond his years. "No one will know."

"What about your friends?" she asked, twirling her bonnet in her hands.

He shook his head. "They will not say a word," he assured her.

Ellie took a relieved breath, and a shy smile came to her lips. "Thank you."

"You're welcome," he said, returning her smile. Then he stepped back, gesturing at the path ahead. "Shall we?"

Ellie nodded and fell into step beside him. Brushing her blond curls back, she fastened her bonnet, keeping the sun out of her eyes.

He glanced down at her. "May I ask your name?"

"Ellie," she whispered and met his eyes, feeling a warmth spread to her cheeks that she could not blame on the sun.

He smiled. "I'm Rick."

For a long time, they walked in silence, a silence that felt comfortable as though they had known each other for a long time.

When the hedges of the estate's garden finally came in sight, Ellie whispered, "Will you tell my mother?"

He shook his head, and relief flooded her body. "I would not dare bring any harm upon you," he said looking down at her.

Again, Ellie felt herself blush. "Thank you."

"She is highly critical of you, is she not?"

Ellie nodded. "She counts my faults on a daily basis."

Rick smiled. "That shouldn't take her long." As they stopped by the long hedge, running along the gardens, his eyes shifted to hers. "I cannot find a single one."

Again, Ellie felt herself blush and quickly averted her eyes.

"You should go," he said, "before anyone sees us together."

Nodding, Ellie smiled at him, then turned and headed back toward the noise of the garden party. Although she was tempted, she did not dare turn around to see if he was still there. Even if she could not see him, she still felt his eyes on her, watching over her safe return.

Frederick Lancaster, she mused. He would be a wonderful man one day. Ellie was sure of it. After all, he had saved her from her mother's wrath, and in her world, there was no greater or more heroic deed than that.

Series Overview

FORBIDDEN LOVE SERIES

HAPPY EVER REGENCY SERIES

THE WHICKERTONS IN LOVE

    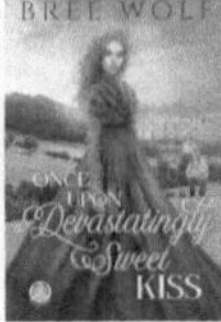  

For more information visit www.breewolf.com

About Bree

USA Today bestselling and award-winning author, Bree Wolf has always been a language enthusiast (though not a grammarian!) and is rarely found without a book in her hand or her fingers glued to a keyboard. Trying to find her way, she has taught English as a second language, traveled abroad and worked at a translation agency as well as a law firm in Ireland. She also spent loooong years obtaining a BA in English and Education and an MA in Specialized Translation while wishing she could simply be a writer. Although there is nothing simple about being a writer, her dreams have finally come true.

"A big thanks to my fairy godmother!"

Currently, Bree has found her new home in the historical romance genre, writing Regency novels and novellas. Enjoying the mix of fact and fiction, she occasionally feels like a puppet master (or mistress? Although that sounds weird!), forcing her characters into ever-new situations that will put their strength, their beliefs, their love to the test, hoping that in the end they will triumph and get the happily-ever-after we are all looking for.

If you're an avid reader, sign up for Bree's newsletter on www.breewolf.com as she has the tendency to simply give books away. Find out about freebies, giveaways as well as occasional advance reader copies and read before the book is even on the shelves!

Connect with Bree and stay up-to-date on new releases:

facebook.com/breewolf.novels
twitter.com/breewolf_author
instagram.com/breewolf_author
amazon.com/Bree-Wolf/e/B00FJX27Z4
bookbub.com/authors/bree-wolf